MARVEL

ANT-MAN

The Incredible Shrinking Suit

By Chris Strathearn

Inspired by Marvel's *Ant-Man*

Based on the Screenplay by Adam McKay & Paul Rudd

Story by Edgar Wright & Joe Cornish

Produced by Kevin Feige

Directed by Peyton Reed

LITTLE, BROWN AND COMPANY
New York Boston

MARVEL
marvelkids.com

© 2015 MARVEL

Little, Brown and Company

Hachette Book Group
1290 Avenue of the Americas, New York, NY 10104
Visit us at lb-kids.com

Little, Brown and Company is a division of Hachette Book Group, Inc.
The Little, Brown name and logo are trademarks of Hachette Book Group, Inc.

The publisher is not responsible for websites (or their content) that are not owned by the publisher.

First Edition: June 2015

Library of Congress Control Number: 2015937501

ISBN 978-0-316-25668-1

10 9 8 7 6 5 4 3 2 1

CW

PRINTED IN THE UNITED STATES OF AMERICA

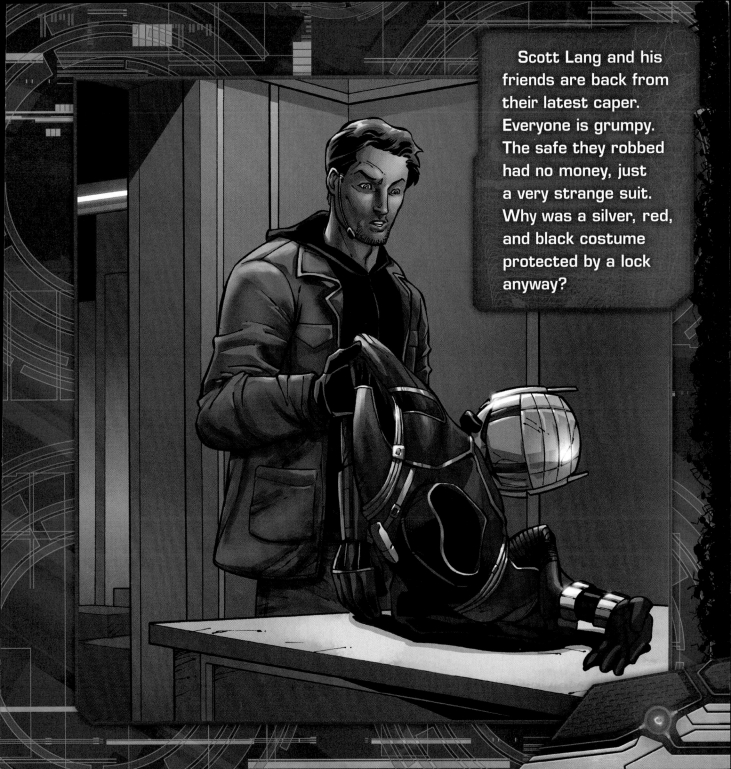

Scott Lang and his friends are back from their latest caper. Everyone is grumpy. The safe they robbed had no money, just a very strange suit. Why was a silver, red, and black costume protected by a lock anyway?

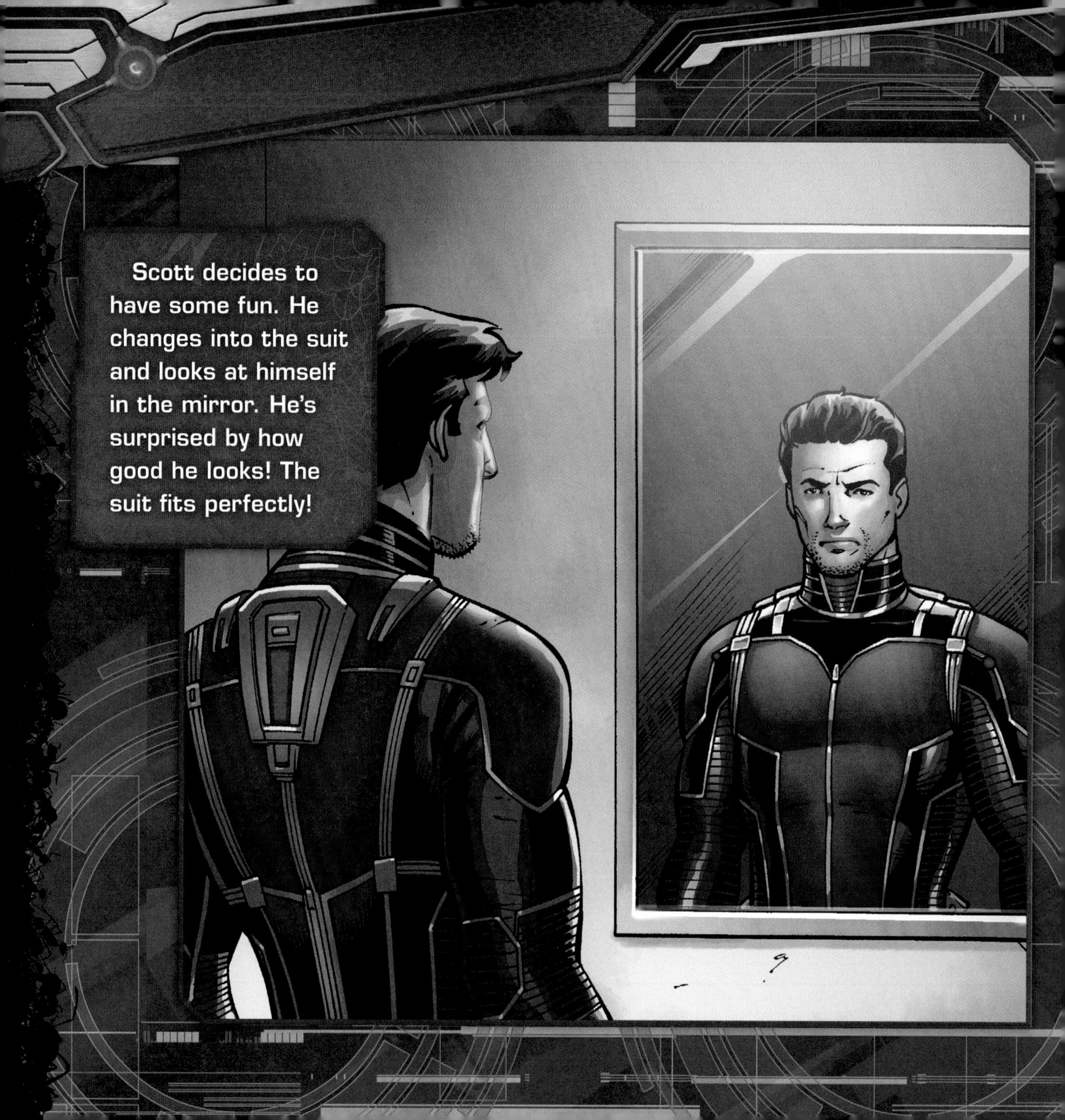

Scott decides to have some fun. He changes into the suit and looks at himself in the mirror. He's surprised by how good he looks! The suit fits perfectly!

Scott notices a hidden red button on his sleeve. He can't help himself and decides to press it.

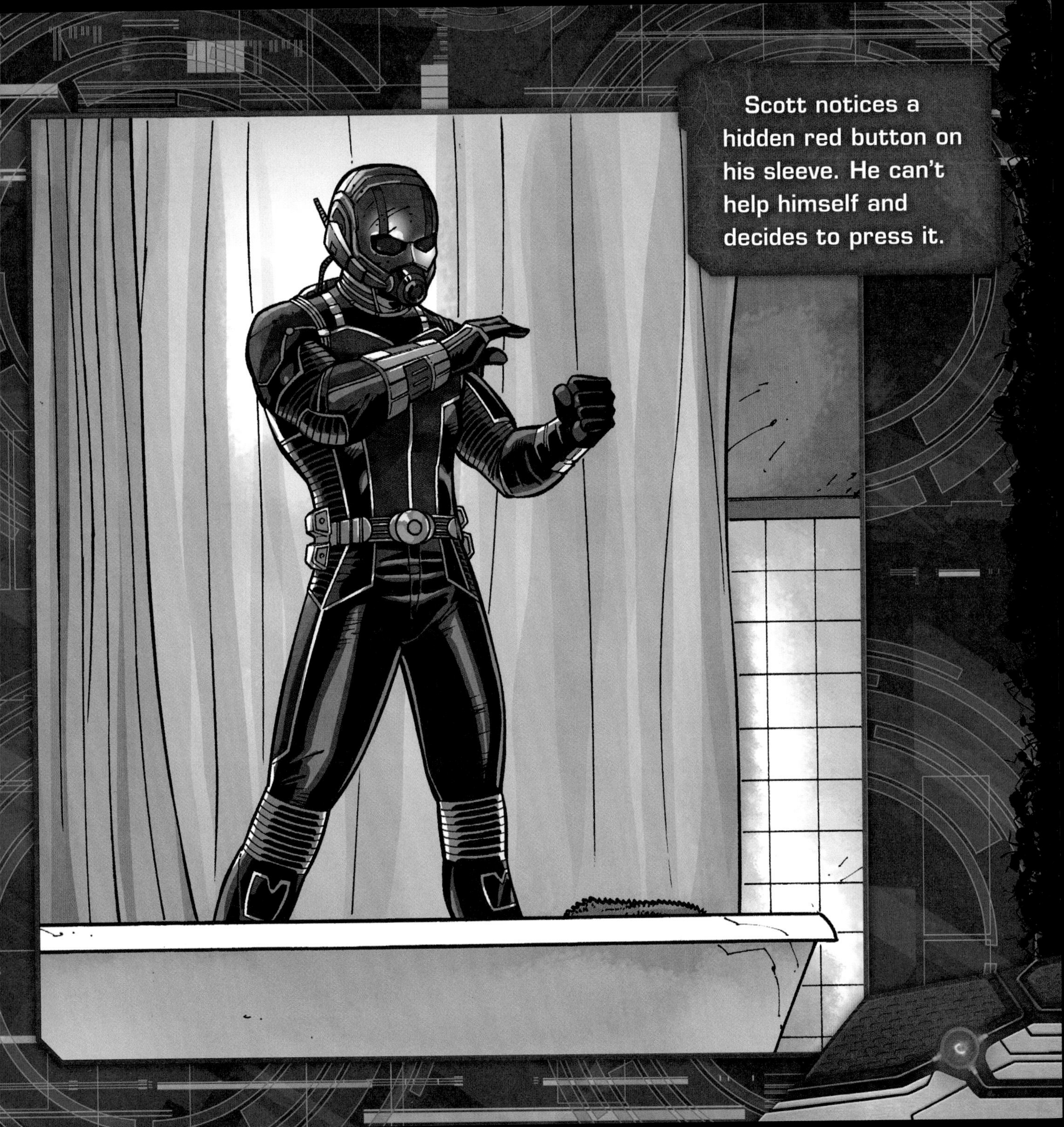

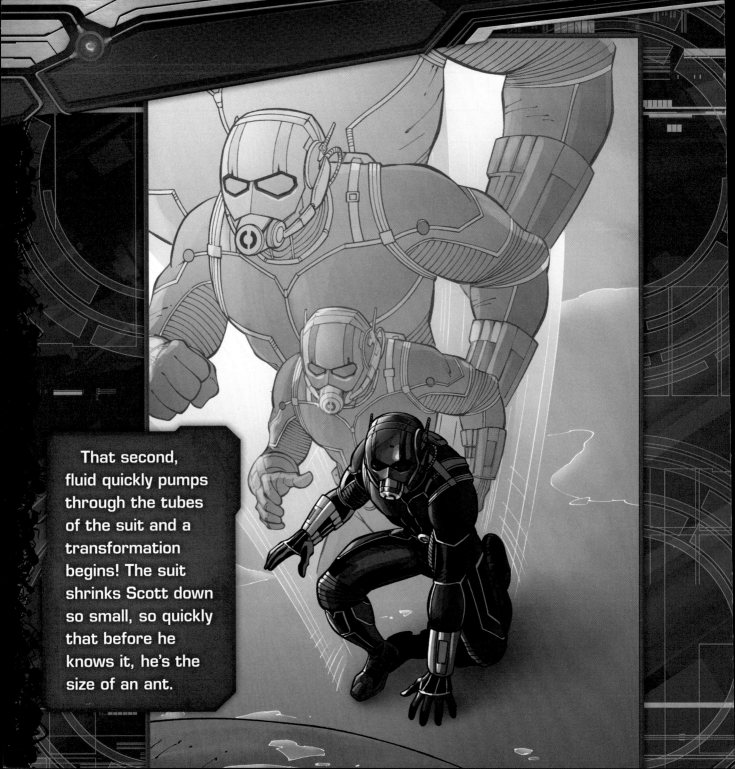

That second, fluid quickly pumps through the tubes of the suit and a transformation begins! The suit shrinks Scott down so small, so quickly that before he knows it, he's the size of an ant.

Looking up, he sees the walls of the bathtub are tall, like a mountain canyon. Scott's roommate comes into the bathroom, but he can't see his miniature friend at the bottom of the tub.

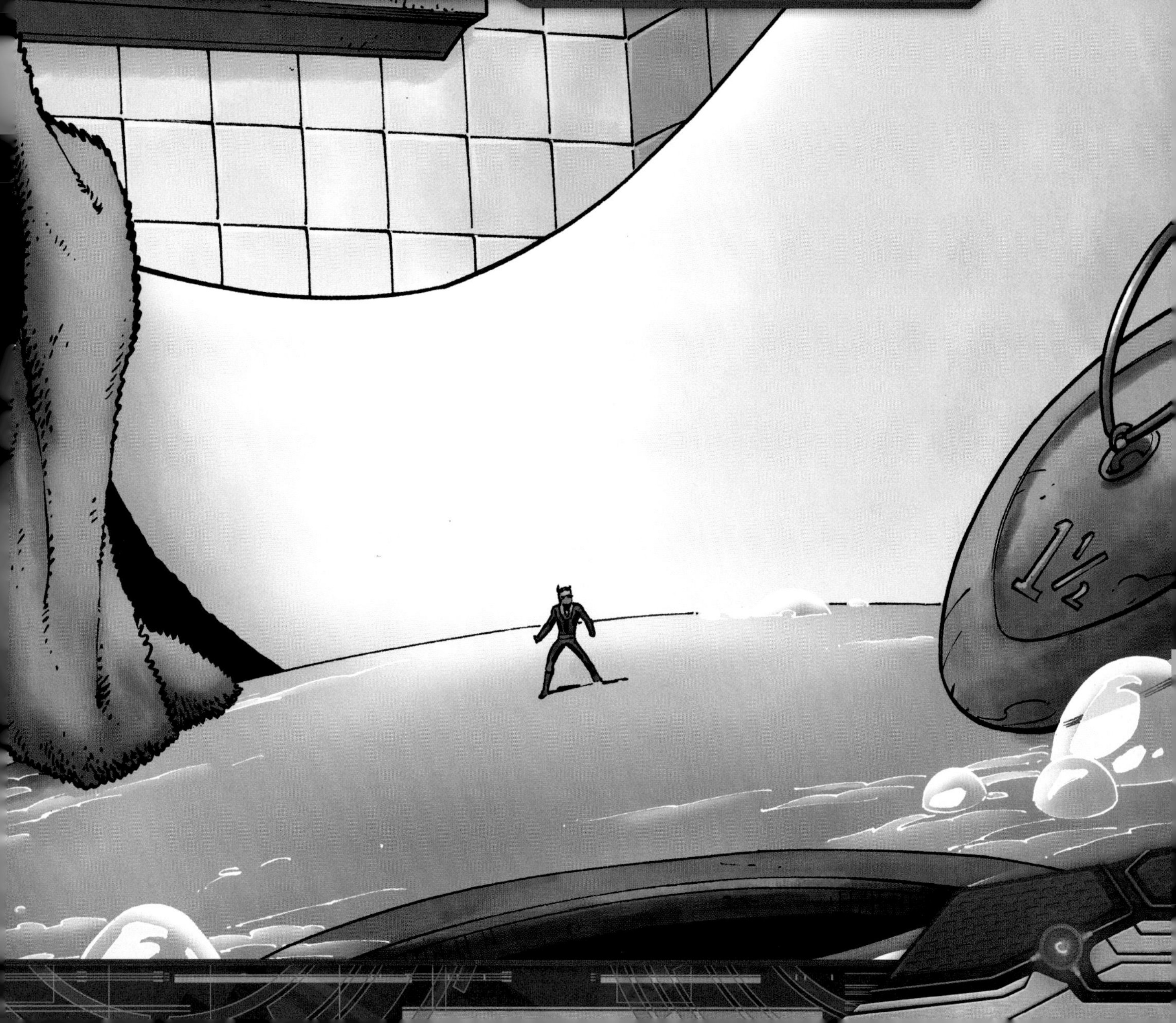
1½

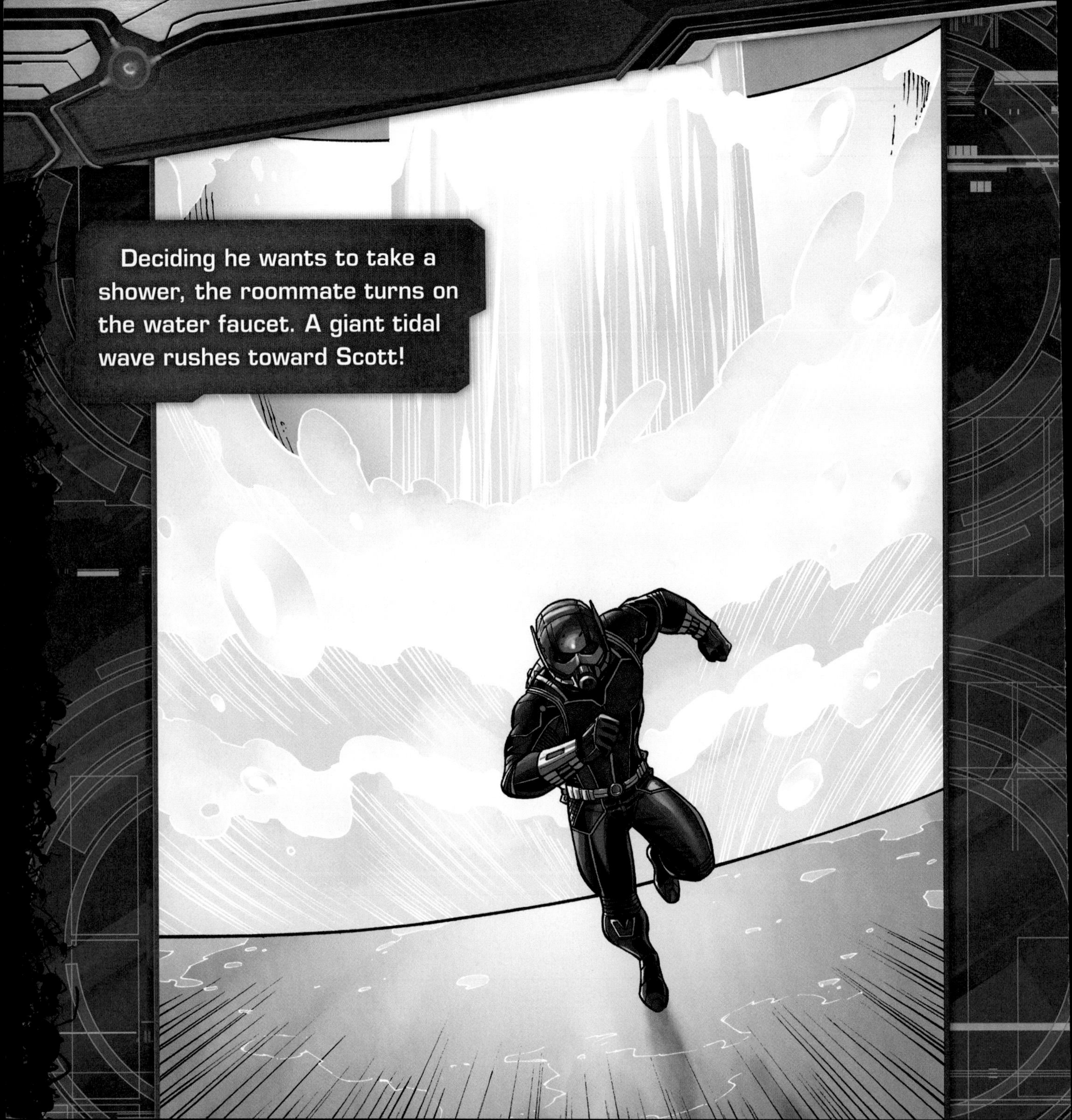

Deciding he wants to take a shower, the roommate turns on the water faucet. A giant tidal wave rushes toward Scott!

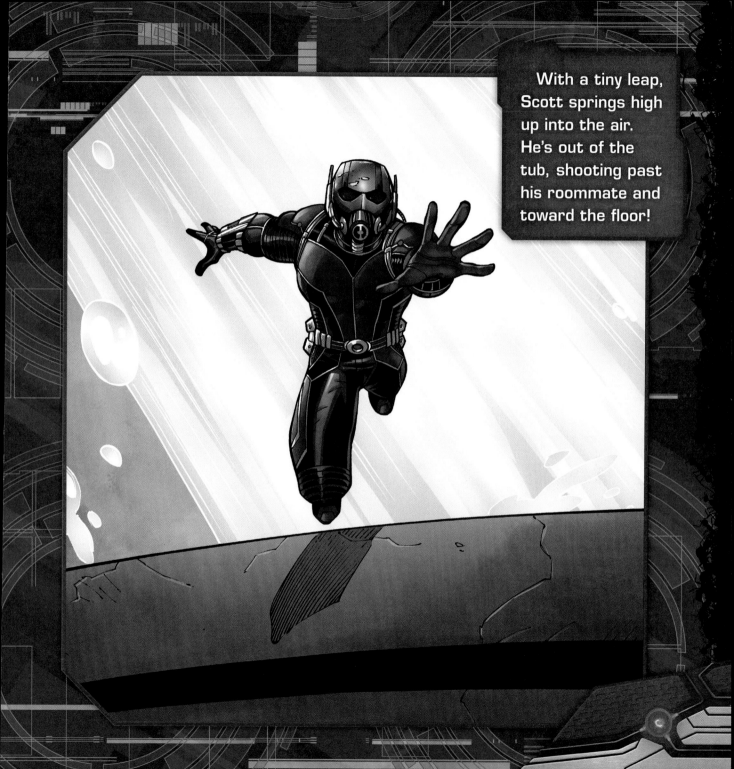

With a tiny leap, Scott springs high up into the air. He's out of the tub, shooting past his roommate and toward the floor!

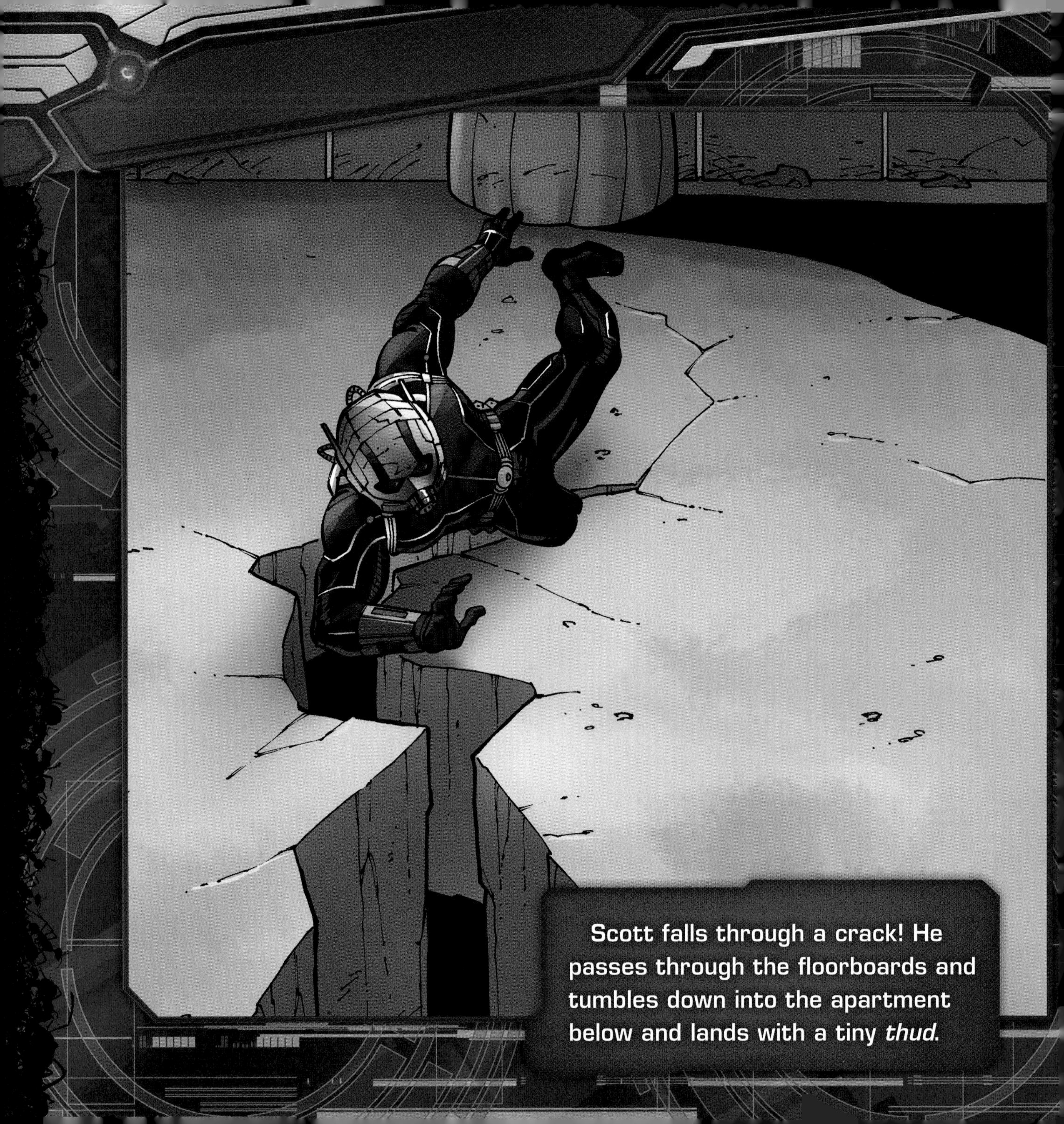

Scott falls through a crack! He passes through the floorboards and tumbles down into the apartment below and lands with a tiny *thud*.

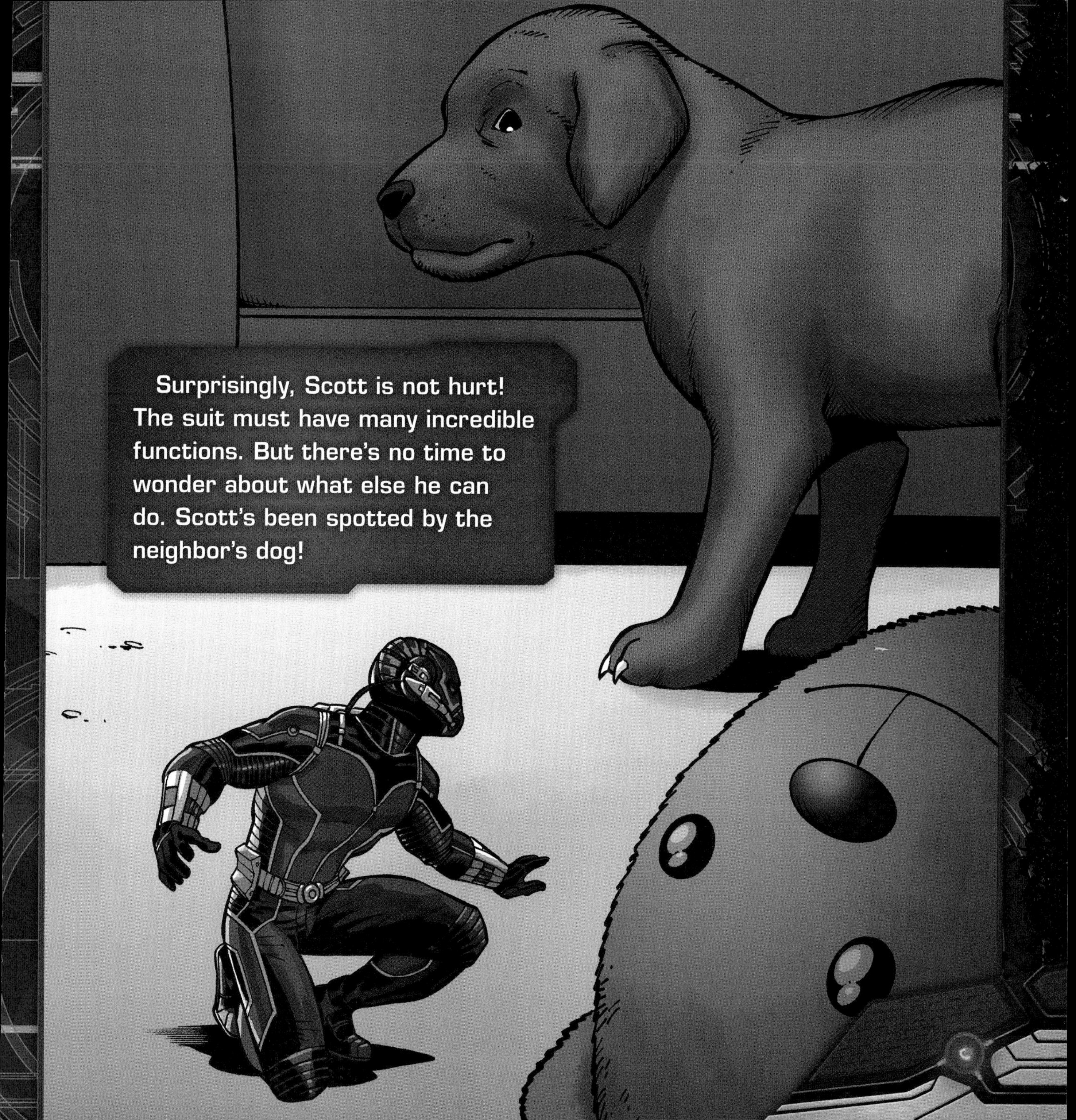

Surprisingly, Scott is not hurt! The suit must have many incredible functions. But there's no time to wonder about what else he can do. Scott's been spotted by the neighbor's dog!

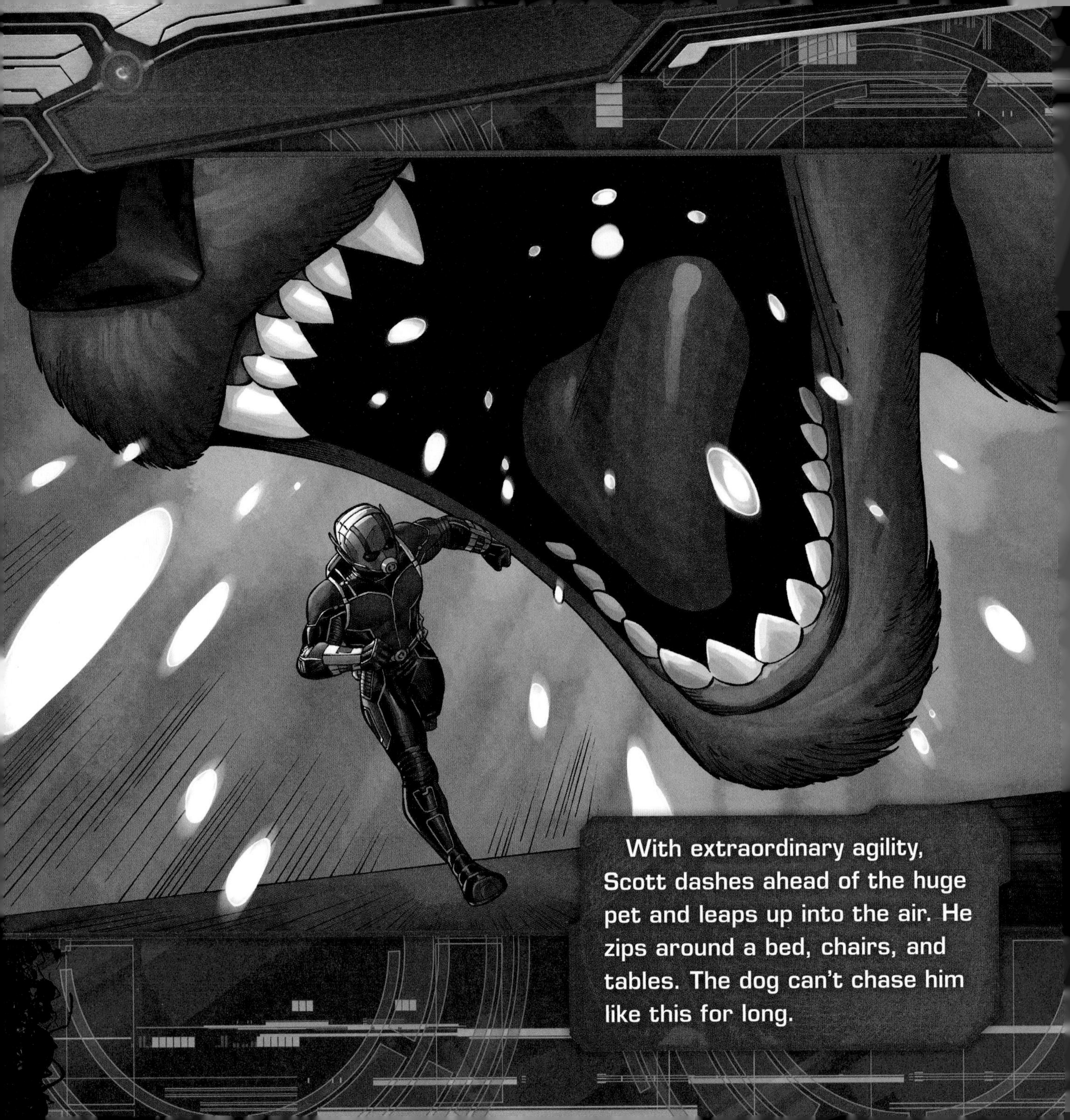

With extraordinary agility, Scott dashes ahead of the huge pet and leaps up into the air. He zips around a bed, chairs, and tables. The dog can't chase him like this for long.

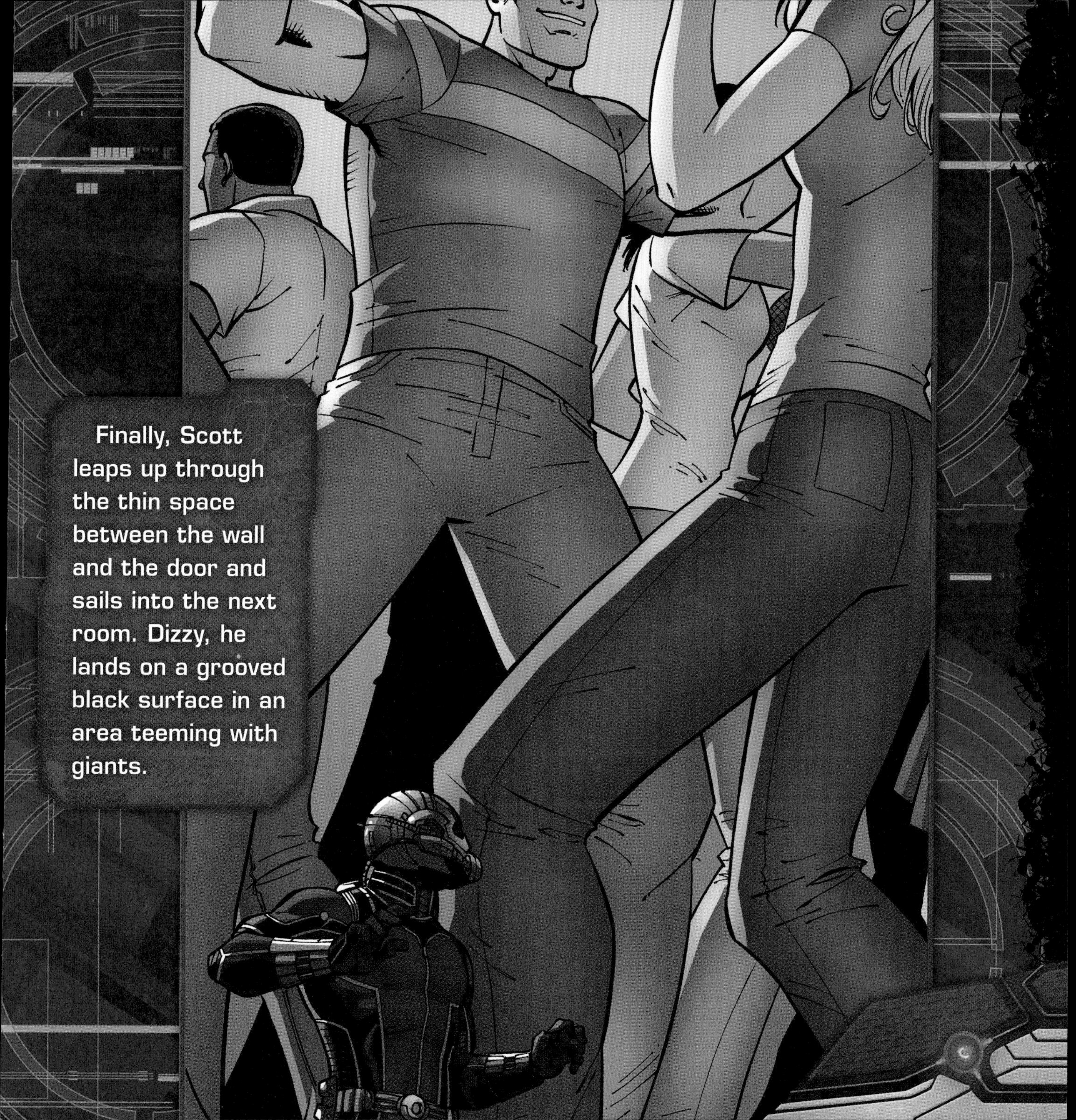

Finally, Scott leaps up through the thin space between the wall and the door and sails into the next room. Dizzy, he lands on a grooved black surface in an area teeming with giants.

The ground is spinning! Scott notices a deadly rod coming toward him. He must run to stay in front of it. He must be on an old record player! The giants must be people dancing! Scott is getting dizzier and dizzier. He must make another leap to get out of this place.

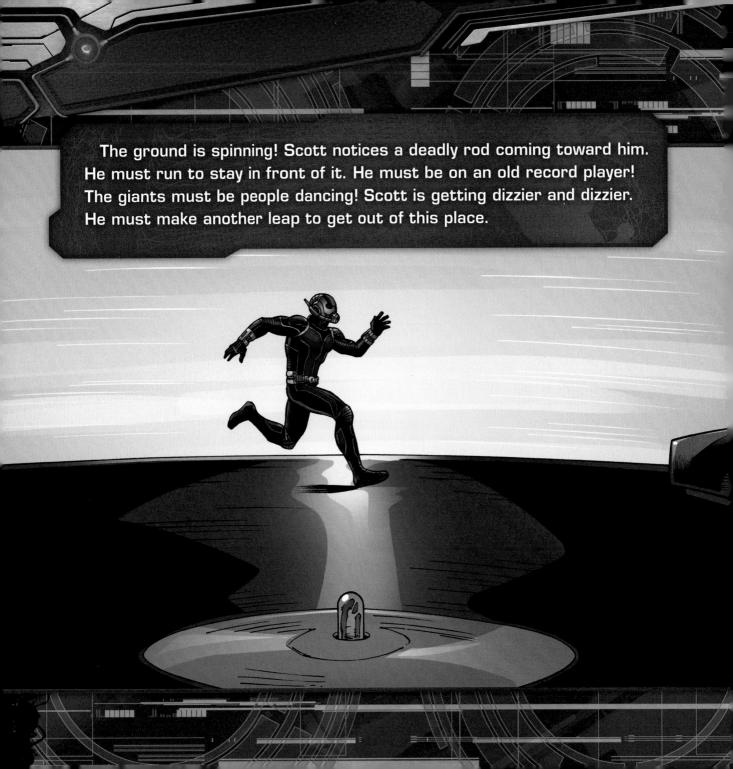

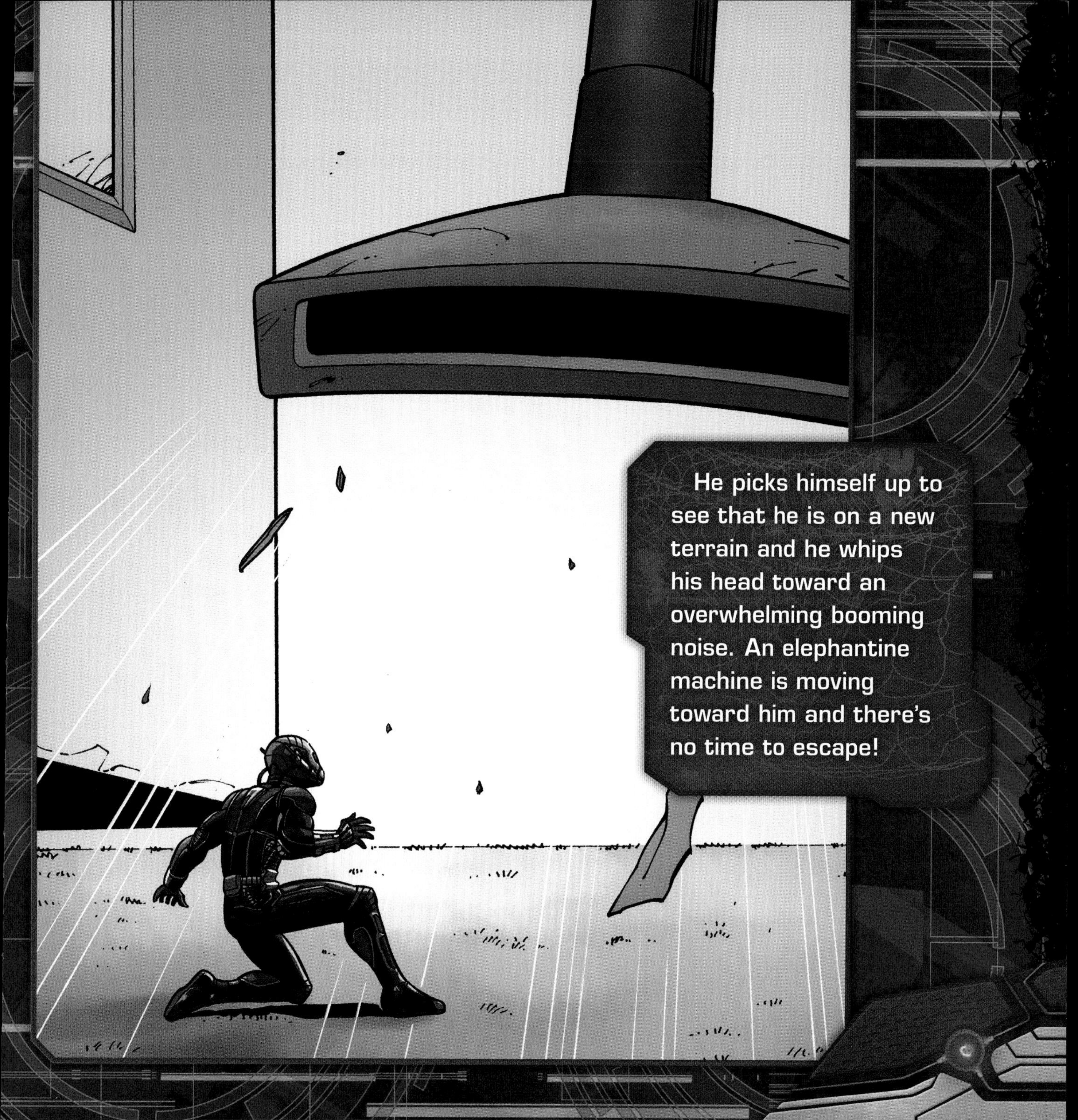
He picks himself up to see that he is on a new terrain and he whips his head toward an overwhelming booming noise. An elephantine machine is moving toward him and there's no time to escape!

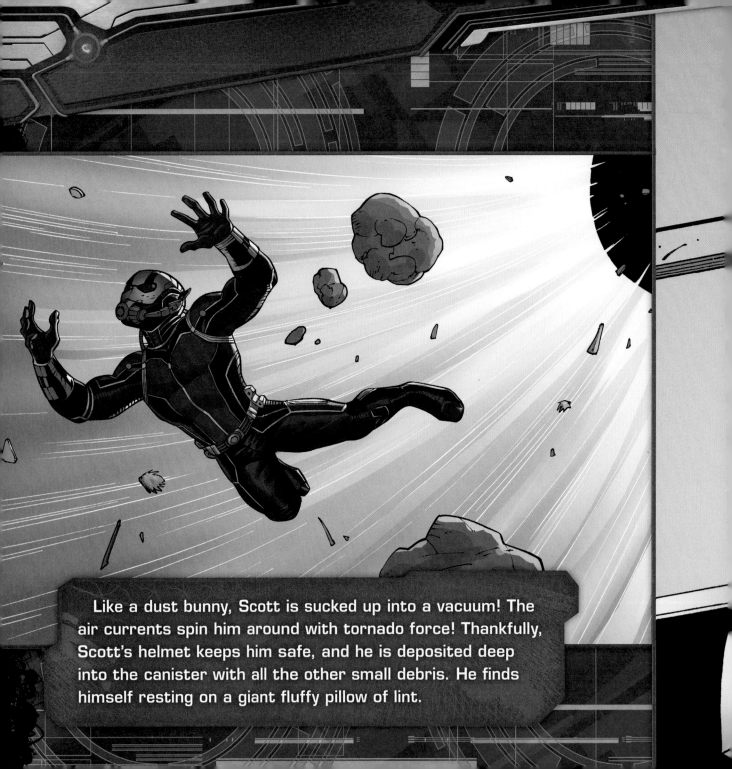

Like a dust bunny, Scott is sucked up into a vacuum! The air currents spin him around with tornado force! Thankfully, Scott's helmet keeps him safe, and he is deposited deep into the canister with all the other small debris. He finds himself resting on a giant fluffy pillow of lint.

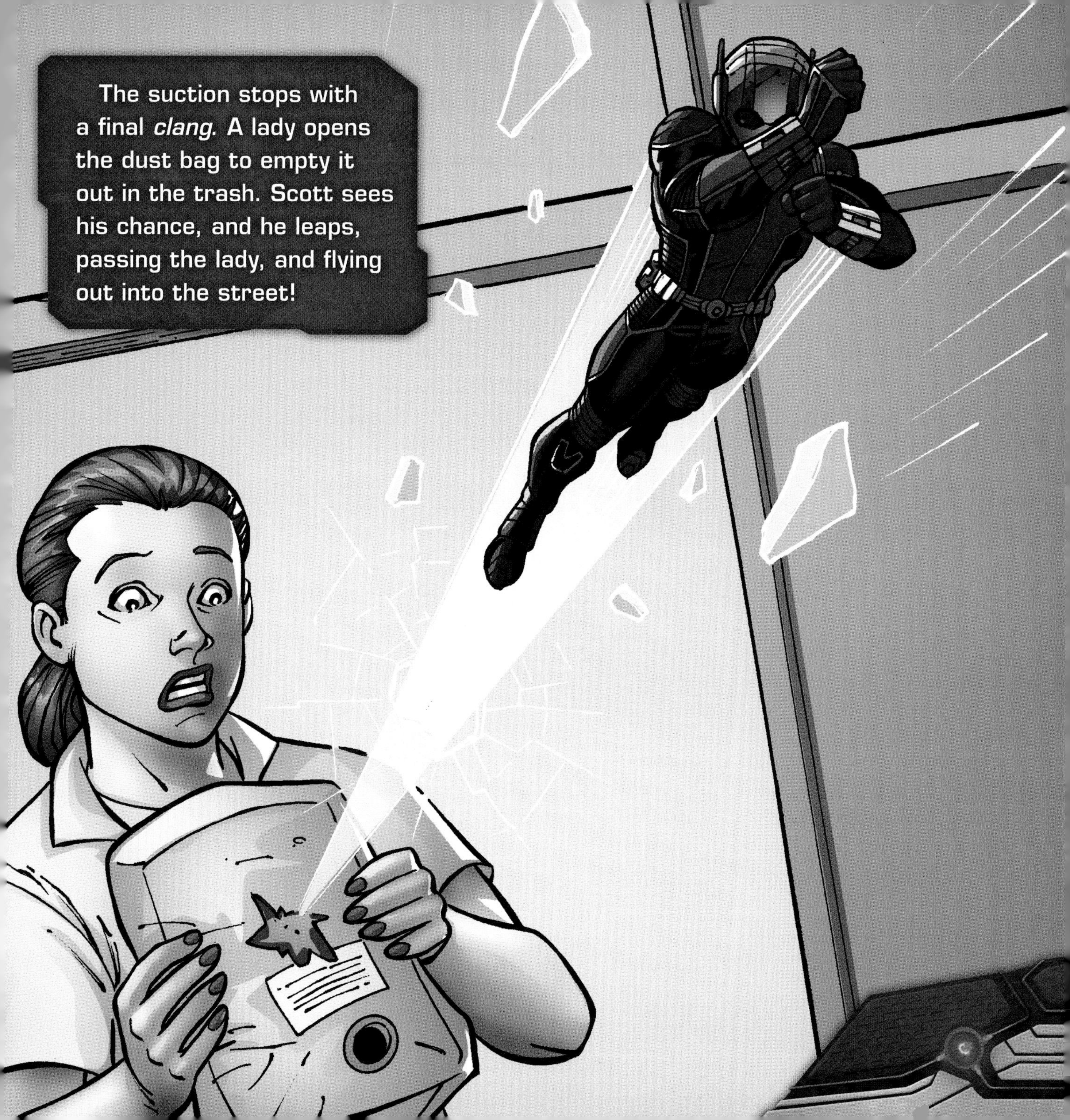
The suction stops with a final *clang*. A lady opens the dust bag to empty it out in the trash. Scott sees his chance, and he leaps, passing the lady, and flying out into the street!

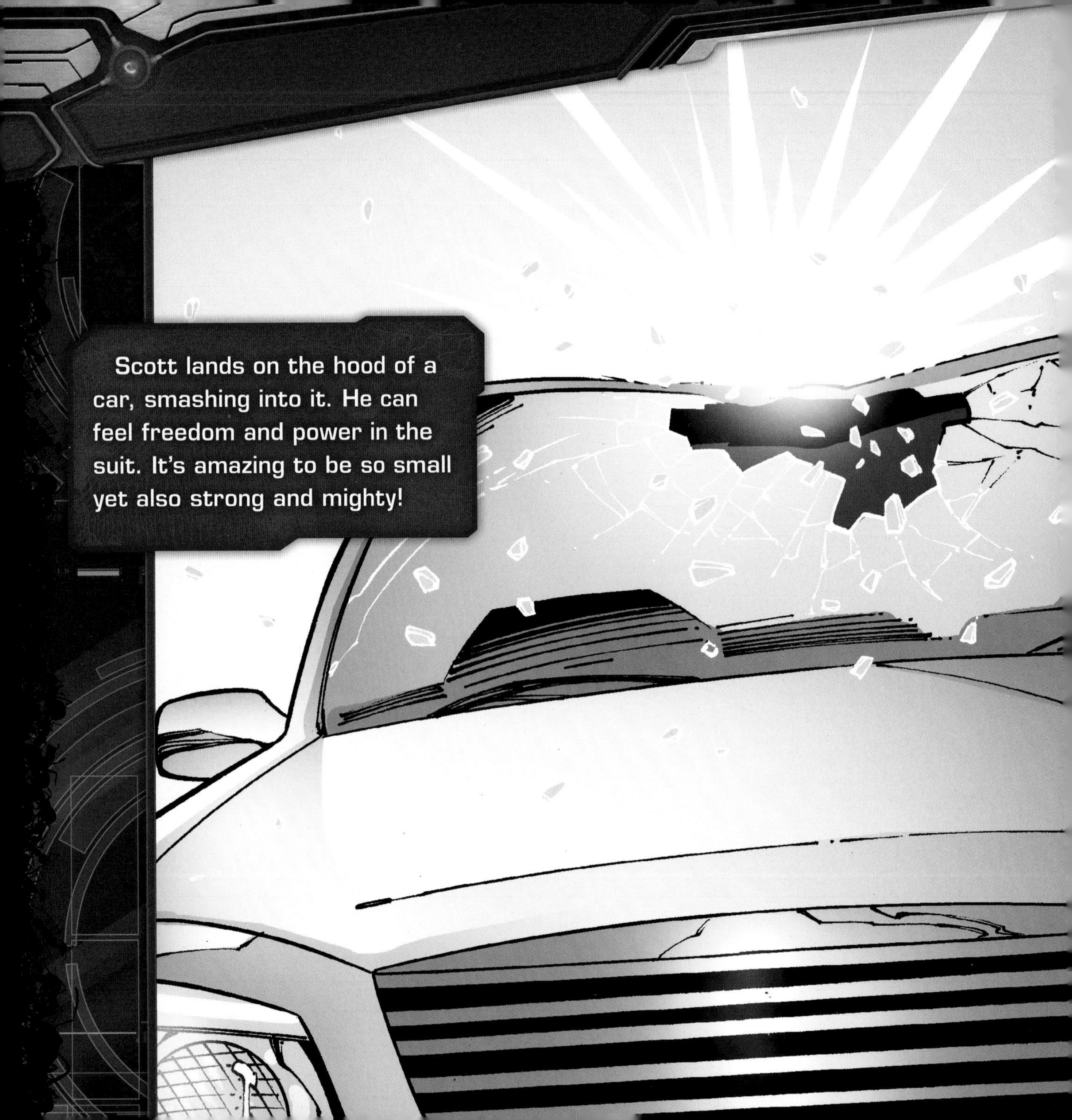
Scott lands on the hood of a car, smashing into it. He can feel freedom and power in the suit. It's amazing to be so small yet also strong and mighty!

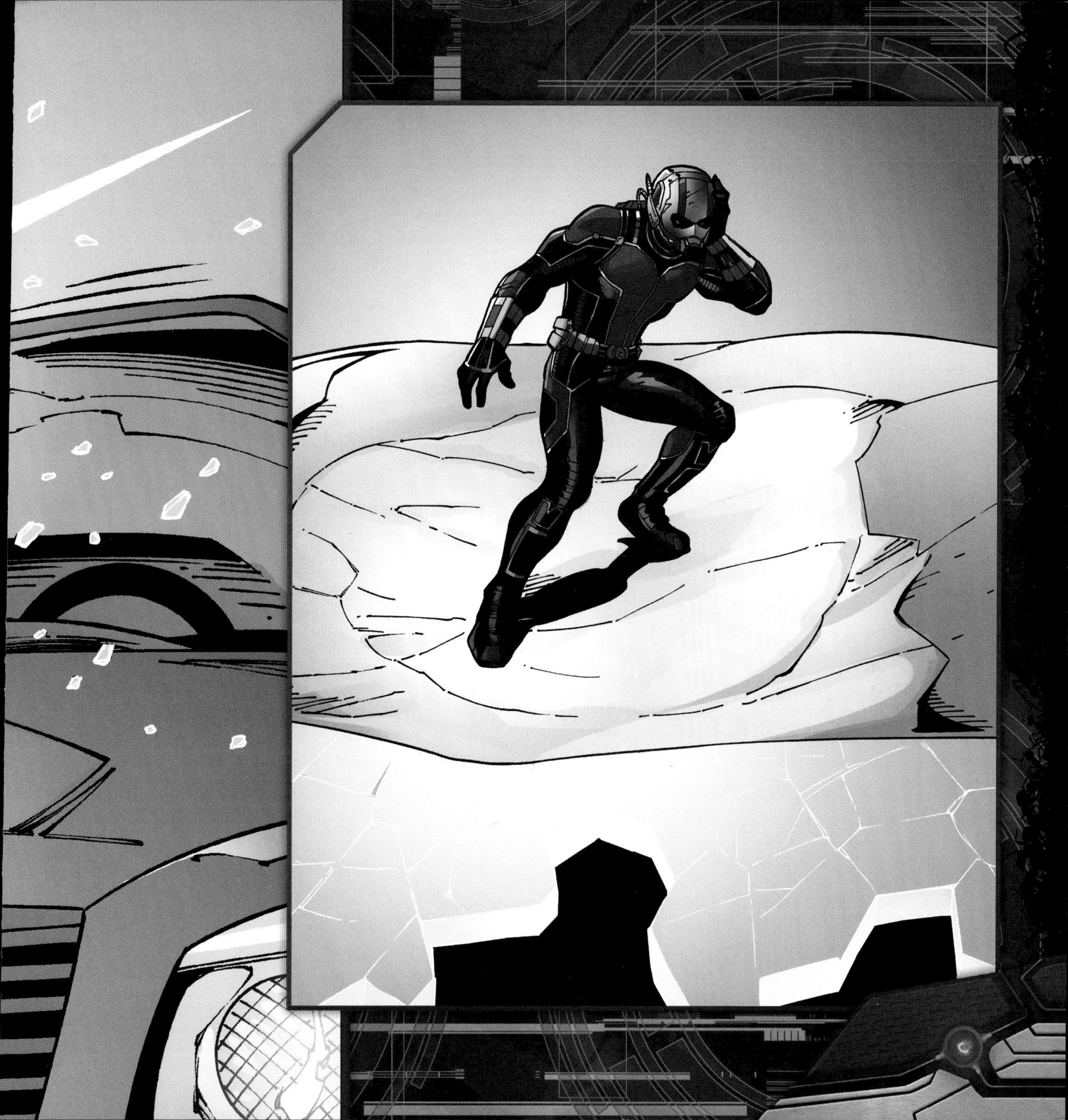

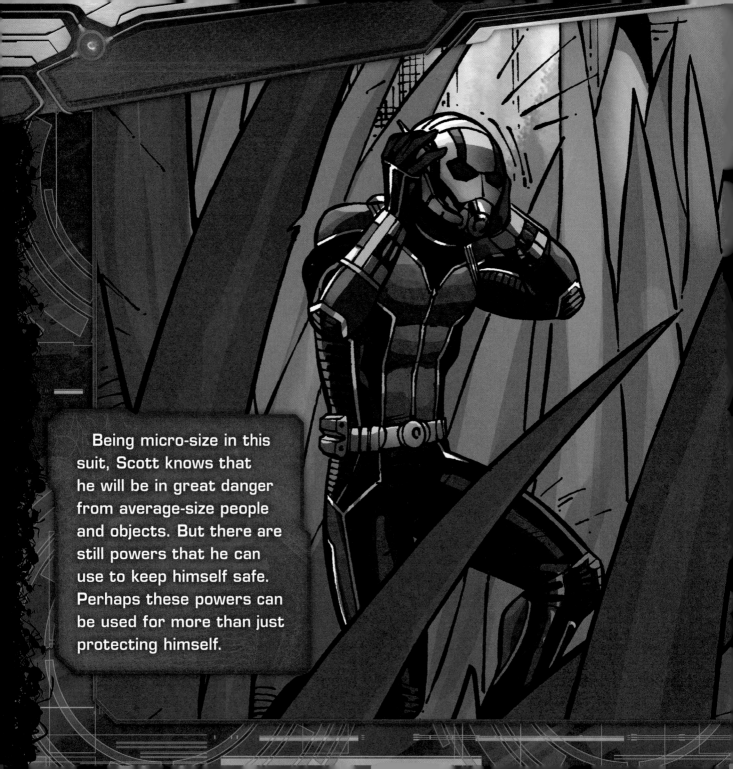

Being micro-size in this suit, Scott knows that he will be in great danger from average-size people and objects. But there are still powers that he can use to keep himself safe. Perhaps these powers can be used for more than just protecting himself.

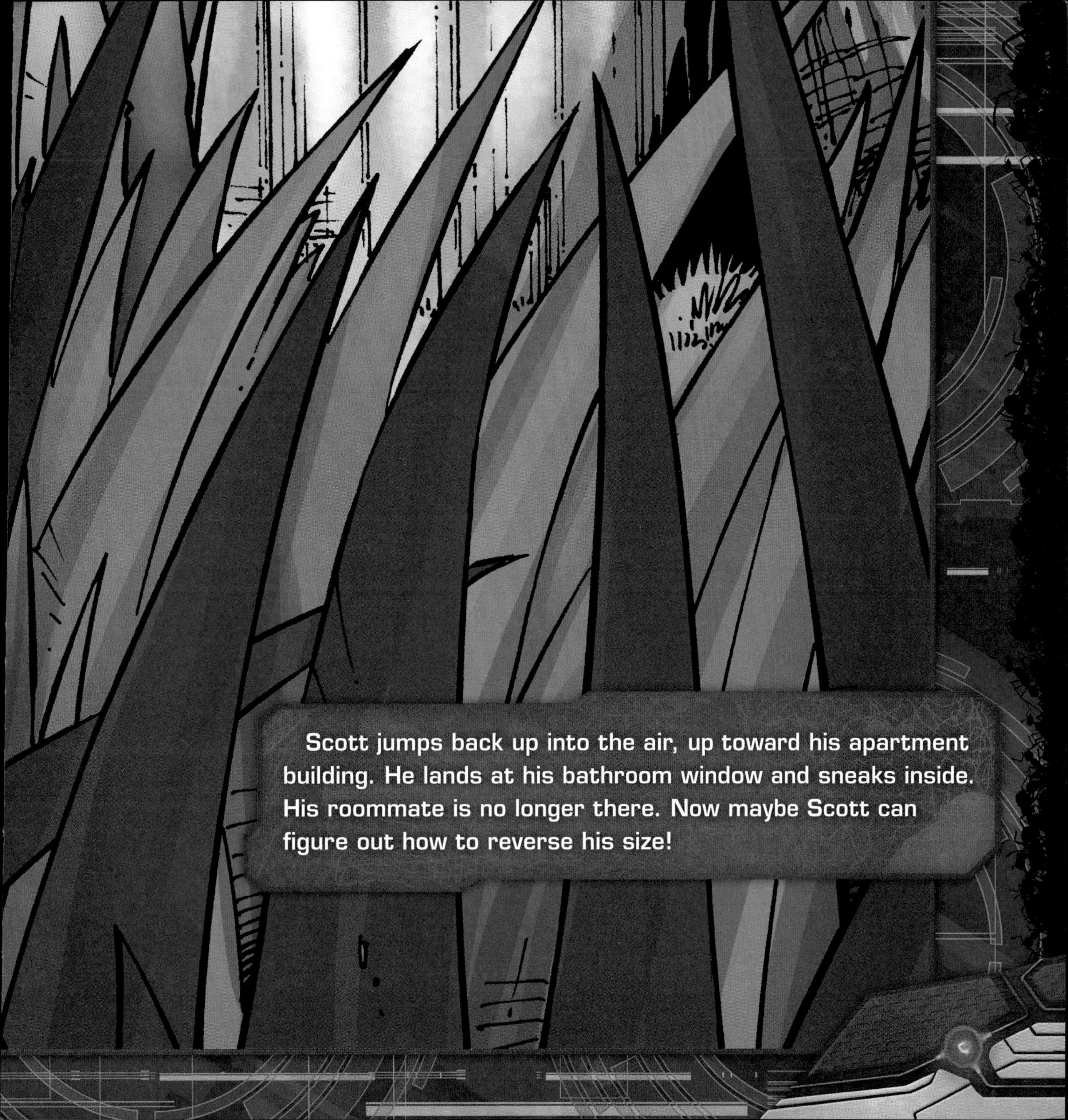

Scott jumps back up into the air, up toward his apartment building. He lands at his bathroom window and sneaks inside. His roommate is no longer there. Now maybe Scott can figure out how to reverse his size!

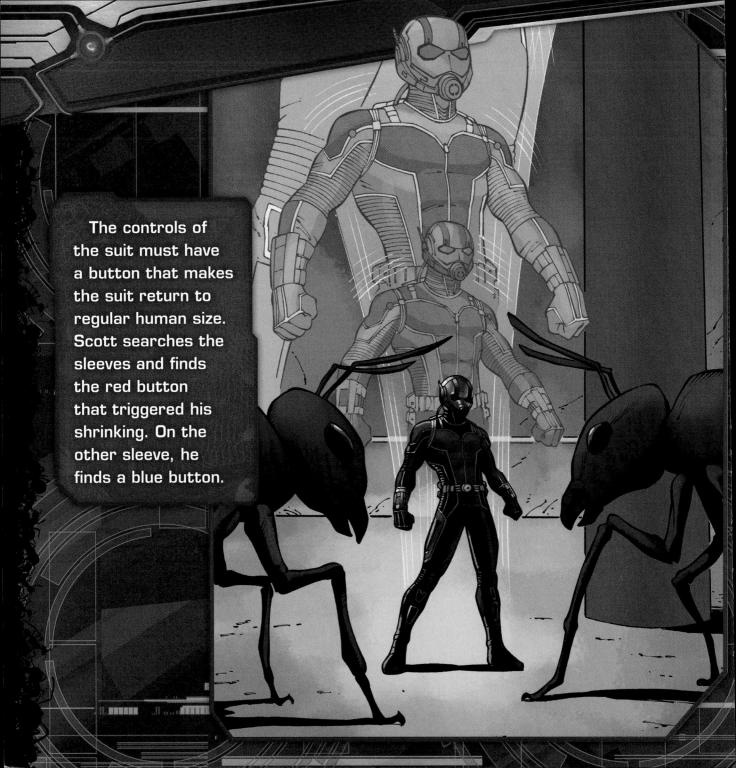

The controls of the suit must have a button that makes the suit return to regular human size. Scott searches the sleeves and finds the red button that triggered his shrinking. On the other sleeve, he finds a blue button.

He presses it, and it triggers the tubes of the suit to change. In an instant, Scott is back to his normal size! Phew!

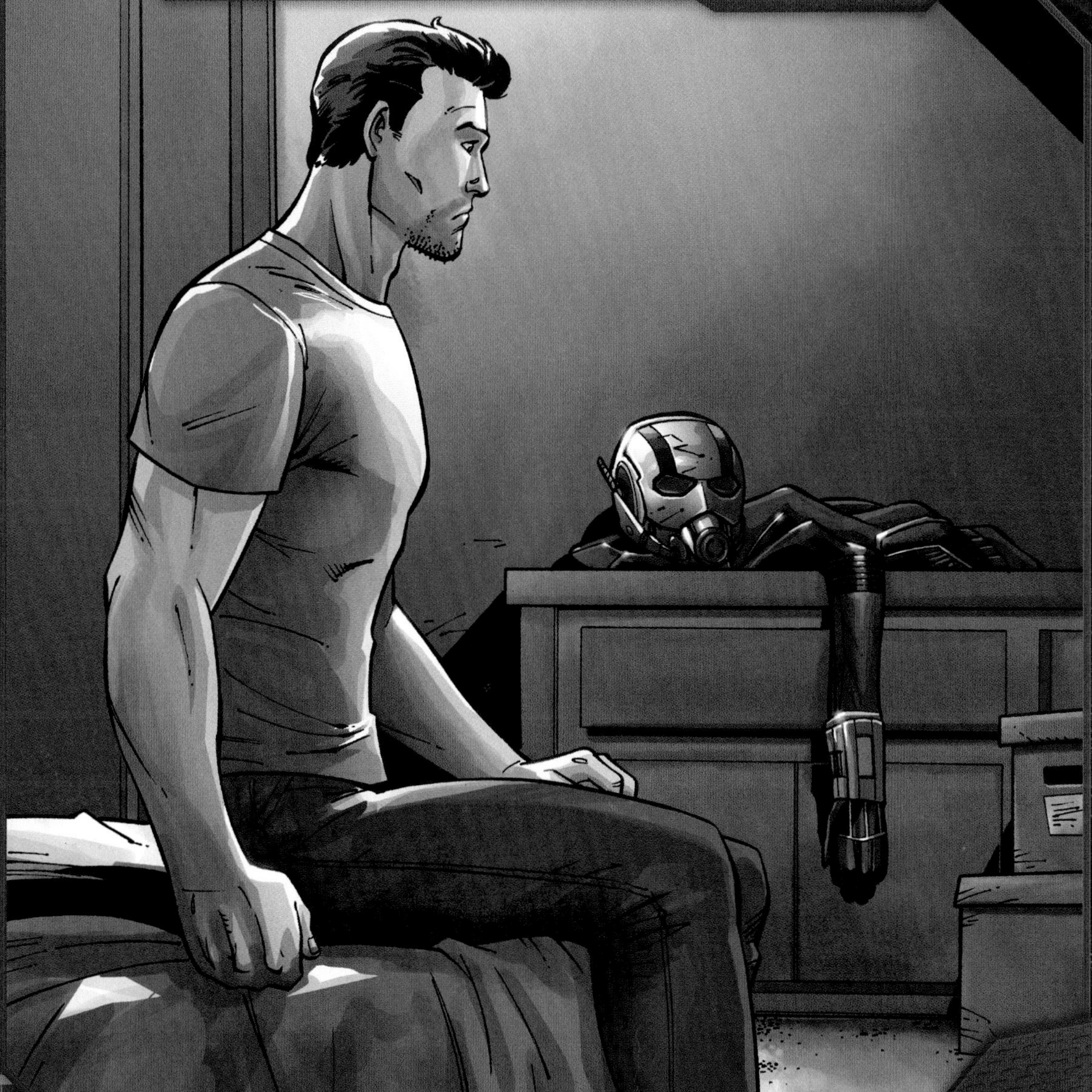

His friends are still in the apartment, but Scott knows he must keep the secret of the suit's power to himself. What will he do now that he can shrink down to miniature size whenever he wants? How will he use the costume's powers? It has super strength and super agility! Whatever he chooses, Scott knows one thing: This will be fun!

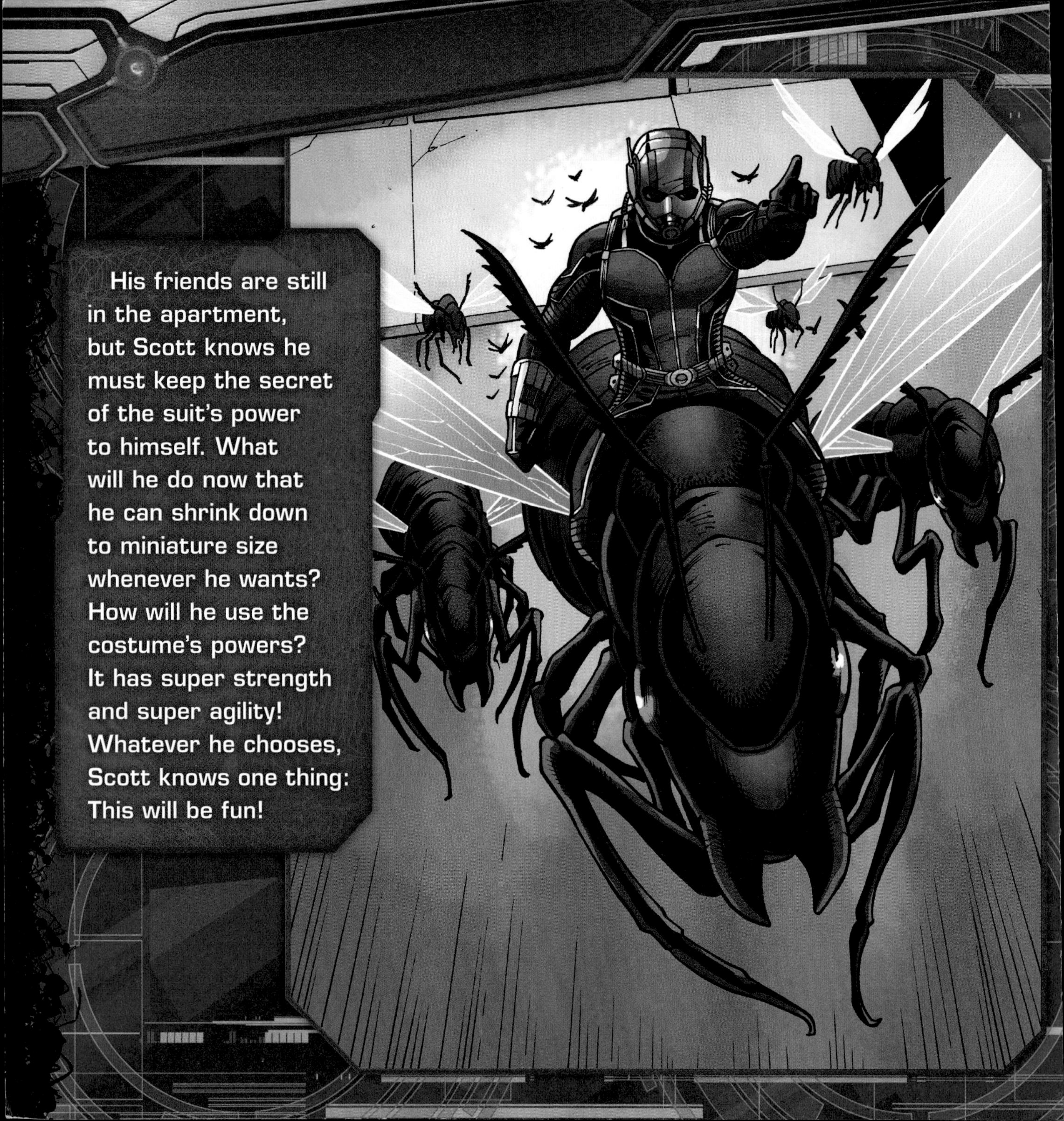